MICHAEL BOND
Paddington
IN TOUCH
Illustrated by Barry Wilkinson

COLLINS COLOUR CUBS

One morning Paddington was opening his mail at breakfast when he came across a letter inviting him to a rugby match.

It seemed the Peruvian Reserves were playing a charity game against his old school, St. Luke's.

Paddington had never been to a rugby match before and he was very excited.

"You can borrow one of my old rattles if you like," said Jonathan.

"It had better work both ways," said Mrs.
Bird. "Don't forget, Paddington's loyalties
will be divided."

"My loyalties will be divided!" exclaimed
Paddington in alarm.

"You won't know which side to cheer on," explained Judy. "Half of you will want St. Luke's to win . . ."

". . . and the other half the Peruvian Reserves," broke in Jonathan.

Paddington considered the matter for a
moment or two over some toast and
marmalade.

"I think," he announced at last, "I'd better have *two* rattles – just to make sure!"

Paddington was as good as his word; when he next appeared he not only had two rattles but he was wearing two brightly coloured scarves as well . . .

. . . and it was an excited party of Browns who set off down Windsor Gardens on their way to the ground.

When they arrived, they found Paddington's friend, Mr. Gruber, had kept some seats for them in the middle of the stand.

"You should have a good view of the game from here, Mr. Brown," he said to Paddington.

Paddington was most impressed. "Fancy having a *sitting* stand, Mr. Gruber," he exclaimed.

Mr. Gruber took a deep breath but, before he had a chance to explain matters, a cheer went up from all around as the two teams trotted onto the field.

Paddington gave them a welcoming burst on both his rattles.

"It's what's known as a compromise," he explained, as Mrs. Brown put her hands to her ears.

"It sounds more like a ghastly noise to me," grumbled Mr. Brown.

But Mr. Brown's remark was lost in the general uproar as the referee blew his whistle and the game began.

For most of the first half Paddington was
kept very busy as first St. Luke's and then
the Peruvian Reserves appeared to be
winning, and his paws began to ache with it
all.

But as the second half got under way an
air of gloom gradually settled over the
ground. It was a hard game and
Paddington's face got longer and longer as
first one and then another of the Peruvian
side was carried off with injuries.

He gave the referee several hard stares through his opera glasses, but he was too far away for them to have any effect.

"Oh, dear," groaned Jonathan, as the whistle went for what seemed like the umpteenth time. "There goes another one. I'm afraid they don't stand a chance now, Paddington."

But Paddington's seat was empty.

"Crumbs!" Jonathan exclaimed. "Where's he got to?"

"Young Mr. Brown seemed to be taking it very much to heart," said Mr. Gruber. "Perhaps he's gone off for a bun."

"Bun nothing!" cried Judy. "Look!" And she pointed towards the centre of the field.

"Now what's he up to?" said Mrs. Brown anxiously.

"Trust Paddington," groaned Jonathan.

Oblivious to the murmurings which spread round the ground, Paddington hurried across the field towards the referee.

"Excuse me," he said, raising his hat politely, "I've come to offer my services to the Peruvian Reserves."

"I'm sorry," said the referee, "but I'm afraid I can't accept them. It has to be someone from the country concerned."

Paddington gave the referee one of his hardest ever stares.

"Well," he said firmly, "I come from Peru – *Darkest* Peru – and I'm *very* concerned."

The man seemed to go a funny colour. He gazed at Paddington and then at the ball.

"All right," he said at last. "You can have a go if you like. After all, it is a charity match and I daresay we can stretch a point."

Paddington needed no second bidding and before the referee had time to change his mind he picked up the ball . . .

. . . and threw it between the legs of the waiting scrum, just as he'd seen the other players do.

Paddington felt very pleased with his first effort at playing rugby and he reached into his duffle-coat pocket for his opera glasses so that he could have a better view of the game.

"Hurry!" shouted Jonathan at the top of his voice. "Run, Paddington . . . run!"

"Oh, dear," said Mrs. Brown. "I do hope he'll be all right."

But, even if Paddington had been able to hear Jonathan's voice above the rest of the crowd, it would have been too late, for the ball suddenly landed back in his paws again.

He looked round for somewhere to put it
and then nearly fell over backwards with
alarm as he saw the rest of the players
thundering towards him.

He wasn't at all sure what happened next, but everything went black as he disappeared beneath a sea of bodies.

Paddington had known rugby was a rough game, but never in his wildest dreams had he pictured it being quite so bad. It felt just as if he'd been trampled on by a herd of wild elephants, and he could see now why so many players had been carried off the field.

But there was worse to come. Just as he was clambering to his feet there came another pounding of feet and a voice shouted "Catch".

"I don't want it, thank you very much!"
he cried in alarm.

But it was too late. Once again the ball
landed fairly and squarely in his paws.

Judy put her hands to her eyes. "I can't bear to watch!" she exclaimed.

"Four points down and only two minutes to go!" cried Jonathan "You can't *not* watch now."

He broke off. "That's funny . . . they seem to have lost the ball."

"What on earth's going on?" said Mr. Brown. "It was there a moment ago."

The Browns weren't the only ones to be puzzled. As Paddington tore off down the field as fast as his legs would carry him the crowd fell silent while the players looked here, there and everywhere for the ball.

One moment it had been in play – the next moment it had disappeared into thin air.

But they hadn't long to wait for an answer. As Paddington arrived on the touch-line the mystery was solved, and a great cheer went up from the crowd of Peruvian spectators behind the goal posts.

"Fancy!" exclaimed Mrs. Bird. "That bear had the ball under his duffle-coat all the time."

"It's a draw! It's a draw!" yelled Jonathan, as the referee blew his whistle for the last time.

"A very fair result in the circumstances," said Mr. Gruber. "I think honour will have been satisfied on all sides – including young Mr. Brown's."

In the confusion that followed, as the Peruvian side came running up in order to be the first to pat him on the back, Paddington struggled to his feet and gazed at the crowd.

Something vaguely familiar had caught his eye as he'd run the last few yards, and he pinched himself several times to make sure he wasn't dreaming.

But Paddington wasn't the only one to feel like pinching himself. Back in the stand Mrs. Bird's sharp eyes were following the direction of his gaze.

"Mercy me!" she exclaimed.

"Gosh!" said Judy. "It can't be."

"It jolly well is!" said Jonathan.

"Will someone *please* tell me what's going on?" said Mr. Brown impatiently.

"Oh, dear, Henry!" exclaimed Mrs. Brown, as two figures drew near. "Look!"

"I'd like to introduce my Aunt Lucy,"
said Paddington. "She's come all the way
from South America with the Peruvian
Reserves Supporters Club and she'd like to
stay for a while."

"That is . . ." he hesitated for a moment,
"that is, if she may?"

For a moment everyone was at a loss for words, then Mrs. Brown recovered herself.

"Of course she may," she said warmly. "We'd love to have her, wouldn't we, Henry?"

"Er, yes," said Mr. Brown. "Er . . . how do you do, Aunt Lucy. Welcome to England."

This story comes from
PADDINGTON ON TOP
and is based on the television film.
It has been specially written by
Michael Bond for younger children.

ISBN 0 00 123540 0
Text copyright © 1980 Michael Bond
Illustrations copyright © 1980 William Collins Sons & Co Ltd.
Cover copyright © 1980 William Collins Sons & Co Ltd.
and Film Fair Ltd./Paddington & Co Ltd.
Cover design by Linda Sullivan.
Cover photographed by Barry Macey.
Printed in Great Britain